Who Will Stop Professor Z?

Disney PRESS
New York • Los Angeles

This is Professor Z.
He is evil.
Who will stop him?

This is Lightning McQueen.
He is racing.
Will he stop Professor Z?

This is Finn McMissile.
He is fighting.
Will he stop Professor Z?

This is Holley Shiftwell.
She is flying.
Will she stop Professor Z?

This is Mater.
He is floating.
Will he stop Professor Z?

This is Professor Z.
Who stops him?

Finn McMissile
stops Professor Z.
Good job!